William's Midnight Adventure and Other Stories

Richmal Crompton, who wrote the original *Just William* stories, was born in Lancashire in 1890. The first story about William Brown appeared in *Home* magazine in 1919, and the first collection of William stories was published in book form three years later. In all, thirty-eight William books were published, the last one in 1970, after Richmal Crompton's death.

Martin Jarvis, who has adapted the stories in this book for younger readers, first discovered *Just William* when he was nine years old. He made his first adaptation of a William story for BBC radio in 1973 and since then his broadcast readings have become classics in their own right. BBC Worldwide have released nearly a hundred William stories on audio cassette and for these international best-sellers Martin has received a Gold Disc and the British Talkies Award. An award-winning actor, Martin has also appeared in numerous stage plays, television series and films.

Titles in the *Meet Just William* series

William's Birthday and Other Stories
William and the Hidden Treasure and Other Stories
William's Wonderful Plan and Other Stories
William and the Prize Cat and Other Stories
William and the Haunted House and Other Stories
William's Day Off and Other Stories
William and the White Elephants and Other Stories
William and the School Report and Other Stories
William's Midnight Adventure and Other Stories
William's Busy Day and Other Stories

All *Meet Just William* titles can be ordered at
your local bookshop or are available by post
from Book Service by Post (tel: 01624 675137).

William's Midnight Adventure and Other Stories

Adapted from Richmal Crompton's
original stories by Martin Jarvis

Illustrated by Tony Ross

MACMILLAN CHILDREN'S BOOKS

First published 2000 by Macmillan Children's Books
a division of Macmillan Publishers Limited
25 Eccleston Place, London SW1W 9NF
Basingstoke and Oxford
www.macmillan.co.uk

Associated companies throughout the world

ISBN 0 330 39212 3

1 3 5 7 9 8 6 4 2

A CIP catalogue record for this book is available from
the British Library.

Typeset by SX Composing DTP, Rayleigh, Essex
Printed and bound in Great Britain by Mackays of Chatham plc, Kent

Contents

Dear Reader

Ullo. I'm William Brown. Spect you've heard of me an' my dog Jumble cause we're jolly famous on account of all the adventures wot me an' my friends the Outlaws have.

Me an' the Outlaws try an' avoid our famlies cause they don' unnerstan' us. Specially my big brother Robert an' my rotten sister Ethel. She's awful. An' my parents are really <u>hartless</u>. Y'know, my father stops my pocket-money for no reason at all, an' my mother never lets me keep pet rats or <u>anythin'</u>.

It's jolly hard bein' an Outlaw an' havin' adventures when no one unnerstan's you, I can tell you.

You can read all about me, if you like, in this excitin' an' speshul new collexion of all my fav'rite stories. I hope you have a jolly gud time readin' 'em.

Yours truly

William Brown

William's Midnight Adventure

William was relieved to hear that his family was not going away for the holidays. William disliked holidays spent away from home. He was not one of those people whose nerves required a frequent change of scene.

He discovered that Mrs Frame, who lived next door, was going away, and had let her house for a month. All William could discover was that the lettee was of the female sex. That told him little. His experience had taught him that while women can be much nicer than men, they can, on the other hand, be much more objectionable.

1

On the whole, he would rather have had a man. You know more where you are with men . . .

Henry and Douglas had been reluctantly dragged to the seaside in the wake of families on pleasure bent. Only Ginger was at home. And Ginger, as untidy and tousled and unwashed as William himself, was, in William's eyes, the ideal companion.

They had raced, and rambled, and scrambled, and wrestled, and climbed trees, and trespassed to their heart's content.

Their internal mechanism, though fortified through the morning by a heavy diet of unripe wild crab apples, unripe hazelnuts, green blackberries and grass (which they chewed meditatively between their more violent pursuits) told them that the luncheon hour was approaching.

Still munching merrily and humming discordantly, they approached William's house. They crept furtively round to the back of it behind the shrubberies.

William did not know what he looked like, but he took it for granted that his appearance was such as to provoke exclamations of horror and disgust from his family.

He was right. His wiry hair stood up as usual in a thick jungle in the midst of which, at a crooked angle, nestled his cap. They had spent part of the morning damming a stream in the meadow with mud. His collar and tie were at the angle they usually attained after a morning of William's normal activities.

William was just going into the potting-shed where he and Ginger were keeping a tin of beetles, when Ginger, who was looking through a hole in the fence, said in a sharp whisper, "I say – I say – she's come!"

William joined him, putting his eye to the hole.

He saw in Mrs Frame's garden a tall woman who was not Mrs Frame. She sat in a chair reading.

William did not see much of her face because it was hidden by a book, so he hoisted himself up and sat on the fence looking down at her. She looked up. He saw a face that did not reassure him – middle-aged and distinctly fierce. She saw – what we have described.

It is only fair to her to say that what she saw did not reassure her either. But William, to do him justice, always made an attempt to establish friendly relationships.

"Hello," he said. "I live here. Next door."

She looked at him as though he were surely part of a nightmare and must vanish if she looked at him long enough. But no, he stayed

there. This dreadful apparition was real and it said it lived next door. Horror and disgust settled upon her face.

"You impertinent little boy!" she said. "Go away! Get down!"

William was a stern lover of justice. "I'm not in your garden," he said judicially, "an' I s'pose we join at this fence. You've got half an' we've got half. Well, I'm sittin' on our half. I wun't mind you sitting' on your half an' I don' see why—"

"Get – DOWN!"

William got down.

"Did you hear that?" he said to Ginger. "Won't let me even sit on jus' our bit of the fence. Thinks it's all hers. If I knew a policeman I'd jus' go an' ask him about it. I bet you could get put in prison for doin' that, for not lettin' people sit on their own bits of a fence. Look at cats – cats sit on fences. Is she goin' to stop all the cats in the world sittin' on fences? You'd think from the way she went on that no one was allowed to sit on fences. Well,

I'd jus' like to know what fences is for if folks can't sit on 'em—"

At this point, William's mother saw him from the morning-room window. "William!" she screamed in horror. "Come in and wash your hands and face and brush your hair."

William gave a sigh expressive of philosophic resignation, yelled, "G'bye" to Ginger – who, at the maternal scream, had already begun to make his guilty way out of William's garden – and went indoors.

"I see Mrs Frame's tenant is here," said Mrs Brown at lunch. "She's a Miss Montagu. I must call."

"I wun't if I was you," said William.

"Why ever not?" said his mother.

"Well, if she treats you like what she treats me . . ." He ended with a dark look and attacked his rice pudding with vigour.

That evening came a letter from the new tenant complaining that the noise by William and Ginger in the garden had completely (underlined) spoilt her afternoon's rest which was most (underlined) important to her health.

The next morning came a letter saying that William's singing in his bedroom in the early (underlined) morning was not only audible to her, but had given her a headache (underlined) from which it would probably be many days before she recovered.

In the evening came another note to demand that William should not be allowed to look over the fence at her, as the sudden appearance of the boy's head had a most disastrous (underlined) effect upon her nerves. She added that if these persecutions (underlined) continued she would be obliged to consult her legal adviser.

William spent the next day with Ginger roaming far afield in search of adventure.

But a note arrived in the evening to say that the boy's whistling as he passed her house was so penetrating (underlined) that she had been obliged to shut all (underlined) the windows at the front of the house, and her health had suffered considerably (underlined) as fresh air was essential (underlined) to it.

William's father divided his wrath impartially between the absent Miss Montagu and the present William. The present William came off the worst.

The auction sale was William's idea. He had attended an auction sale with his uncle the week before, and his uncle had purchased a "lot" which included two small pictures of so hideous execution and design that he had generously presented them to William.

William, who had been thrilled and surprised by the proceedings of an auction sale, decided to dispose of his two pictures by auction, and invited a select band of potential bidders to his garden.

"We won't make a noise," said William to his mother. "We won't disturb her. We'll do it all in whispers."

Mrs Brown went indoors hoping for the best. Mrs Brown spent most of her time hoping for the best. From her, William had inherited some of his glorious optimism.

The potential bidders arrived. They were not representative of William's friends. Most of William's friends were away. These were merely a varied collection of such of his schoolfellows as he could muster. Most of them would in normal times have been beneath his notice on the score of extreme youth.

They sat down on the grass in William's back garden and stared around them suspiciously.

William stood behind the upturned wheelbarrow on which were the two pictures and held a gardening fork to represent the hammer. Ginger stood next to him.

William held up one of the pictures. It was about ten inches square and represented a female with incredibly long hair and incredibly flowing robes, chained to a stake on a lonely seashore. She was simpering coyly at the spectators out of her ornate frame. It was called *The Martyr*.

"Ladies an' gentleman," began William,

"first of all we're goin' to sell this picture."

"Whaffor?" said a very small person of the female sex who was sitting on the grass.

William turned on her a glance that should have annihilated her utterly. "What do you mean – whaffor?" he said contemptuously. "Why shun't we sell a picture?"

"Why should you?" said the small female, quite unannihilated.

William felt nonplussed. No one at the auction sale he had attended with his uncle behaved like this. He decided to take the line of the high hand. "We shall sell," he said loftily, "'xactly what we like. We shall sell – camels if we want to."

Camels was an inspiration. He felt that camels was rather good. He prepared to go on with the sale.

"Ladies an' gentlemen—" but the small female, who had been deeply considering his last remark, burst forth again.

"Camels! Whaffor d'you want to sell camels?"

"First of all," went on William, "we're goin' to sell this picture. First of all, ladies an' gentlemen, take a good look at this picture."

"Who wants to buy camels?" said the small female passionately. "What's the good of sellin' 'em?"

"Jus' look at this picture," went on William. "It's prob'ly a picture you'll never see again – you'll never again have a chance of buying a beautiful picture like this cheap."

"Anyway," said the small female, looking round the garden with the air of one deliver-

11

ing a crushing argument, "where are your camels? Why don't you bring out 'em and start sellin' 'em, instead of talkin' about 'em?"

"Kin'ly stop int'ruptin'," said William, "We've not come here to listen to you. We've come here to sell these things. Ladies an' gentlemen, this picture is one of the most beautiful pictures in the world. If you'll jus' look at it for a few minutes—"

A very small boy in the front suddenly burst into tears. "Wanter buy a camel!" he sobbed.

The small female encircled him with tiny motherly arms and turned an indignant glance upon William. "Now look what you've done, you nasty, cruel boy," she said. "You've made him cry. Well, where are your camels you keep talking about?"

"I don't keep talking about 'em, I never said I had any camels."

The small female opened eyes and mouth in horror. "Oh!" she gasped. "You did. Oh, you storyteller!"

The small boy's wails increased in volume.

"Want a camel," he yelled as the tears ran down his cheeks.

"You jus' don' know how to act at auction sales," stormed William indignantly. "I'm tryin' to sell pictures an' here you keep carryin' on about camels."

At this point the proceedings were interrupted by the arrival of Mrs Brown. She looked pale and harassed and carried a note in her hand. "Oh, William," she said, "how could you? She's written again. She says that the noise is ear-splitting and that her nerves can't stand it. She says," – she turned the note over helplessly – "she says a lot of things all underlined and, oh, William, you did promise to be quiet."

"I *was* bein' quiet," said William, "Then they all start talkin' about camels, an' I can't stop 'em makin' a noise."

William and Ginger sat disconsolately on the still upturned wheelbarrow. The spectators of the auction sale had indignantly departed, the small boy still wailing pitifully.

"What'll we do now?" said Ginger, looking down with distaste upon the two pictures that shared the wheelbarrow with them.

"Somethin' quiet," groaned William. "Let's play ball."

William fetched a ball and threw it to Ginger. Ginger caught it and threw it to William. William missed it and it went over the fence into Miss Montagu's garden.

William fetched another ball, and threw it to Ginger. Ginger missed it and it went over the fence into Miss Montagu's garden.

Ginger went home and got his ball. He threw it to William. They threw it to each other and caught it ten or eleven times.

Then it went over the fence into Miss Montagu's garden.

William fetched his bow and arrows. The fence by Miss Montagu's garden was the only place to fix the target. Every other side of the garden consisted of flowerbeds.

They shot busily at the target for ten minutes. At the end of the ten minutes all their arrows were in Miss Montagu's garden.

"Well," whispered Ginger gloomily, "what we goin' to do now?"

William, with all his faults, never lacked courage. He hoisted himself upon the fence to survey cautiously the enemy's ground. He was somewhat taken aback to meet the stern gaze of the enemy in person. But even so he was not defeated. He met her gaze unflinchingly and said boldly, "There's a few of our balls an' things come over into your garden. Can I come and gettem, please?"

"No, you may not, you naughty little boy," said the enemy furiously. "I have collected them and I will keep them. Get down."

William deliberately drew his features into a horrible contortion and then descended from his perch. He had been slightly gratified and cheered by the shudder of horror that passed over the face of his enemy at his grimace. It is almost impossible to describe the gargoyle-like masks into which William could twist his countenance.

"Well, what we goin' to do now?" whispered Ginger forlornly.

William looked around. At their feet stood his beloved mongrel.

"Let's wash Jumble," said William, making a grab at the unfortunate animal before the fatal "wash" could send him off like an arrow from a bow. He took off Jumble's collar and hung it carelessly over the fence.

Half an hour later one fairly dry dog and two fairly damp boys emerged from the wash-

shed and made their way over to the fence.

The collar was nowhere to be seen. William again hoisted himself on to the fence and looked down. Again he found himself gazing down into the face of his enemy. His enemy held Jumble's collar in her hand.

"'Scuse me," said William severely, "that's mine. I mean it's Jumble's."

"I found it in my garden," she snapped.

"It must have fell down, then," said William.

"I shall confiscate everything of yours I find in my garden," said the enemy sternly.

She walked indoors. William sat motionless upon his fence. Through the window he could see her enter her dining-room and place Jumble's collar in a cupboard.

He descended from the fence. Upon his freckled frowning face was a set look of purpose.

It was midnight. William, wearing an overcoat and a black mask, climbed cautiously over the fence and crept up Miss Montagu's garden to

Miss Montagu's dining-room window.

In one pocket of his overcoat was his penknife, in the other a handsome pistol which had cost originally one shilling and sixpence, and which figured in most of the Outlaws' adventures.

When he reached the dining-room window he took his penknife out of his pocket and began to attack the catch. It was a catch which an infant burglar could have manipulated in his sleep.

William opened the window and entered Miss Montagu's dining-room. Though sternly bent on what he looked upon as an errand of justice, he was none the less thoroughly enjoying himself in his role.

He opened the cupboard and his eyes beneath the black mask gleamed. There they were: his two balls, Ginger's ball, all his arrows, Jumble's collar . . . With a little snort of triumph he put them all into his pocket.

Then a sound at the door made him turn, and his heart leapt up to the top of his head and then down to the bottom of his boots.

Miss Montagu stood in the doorway clutching a pink dressing-gown about her. William looked round wildly for escape. There was none.

The only alternative to flight was courage. He had recourse to that. He whipped his one-and-sixpenny pistol out of his pocket.

"Hands up," he croaked in a deep bass voice. "Hands up or I fire."

It was a very dark night. All Miss Montagu could see was a vague form behind what was most certainly some sort of revolver. She put up her hands.

"I – I'm unarmed," she said with chattering teeth. "I'm a p-p-poor defenceless woman – think of your wife – think of your s-s-sister – think of your m-m-mother – don't, I beg of you, d-do anything rash."

"Sit down," ordered William.

She sat down. "D-d-do be c-c-careful," she pleaded. "You know sometimes j-j-just an involunt-voluntary movement makes them go

off. I haven't anything really v-v-valuable, I assure you. I— oh, d-d-do be c-c-careful," she screamed as William made a movement with his pistol.

William was backing past her slowly to the open window. At last he reached it.

To his trembling victim, who still held up her hands rather in the attitude of a lap dog in the act of begging, it seemed as if he vanished suddenly and completely into the night.

She made her way unsteadily to the window and peered out into the darkness. There was no sign of him.

The danger was over. It was obviously time for her to faint or have hysterics. But there is something unsatisfactory in fainting or having hysterics without an audience. She rang the bell violently. She screamed "Fire! Murder!" at the top of her voice. Her domestics, in various stages of undress, gathered round her. Then, most effectively and dramatically and carefully, she fainted on to the hearth rug.

Meanwhile, William, in his bedroom

black mask and pyjamas, was dancing a war dance round three balls, a heap of arrows and a dog collar.

William was down in good time the next morning but he found his next-door neighbour already in the dining-room.

"Did you hear nothing?" she was saying excitedly to Mrs Brown. "My house has been ransacked – ransacked from top to bottom. And when I disturbed him – well, I believe there were two or three of them – yes, I'm quite sure there were at least two of them – great big men, my dear Mrs Brown, both wearing masks – they covered me with revolvers."

She became dramatic, and William looked on with great interest. He saw Miss Montagu cover Mrs Brown with an imaginary revolver. Mrs Brown edged behind the sofa.

"They threatened me with instant death if I moved hand or foot," continued Miss Montagu. She advanced threateningly upon

Mrs Brown, the imaginary revolver in her hand. Mrs Brown sat down, shut her eyes, and gave a little scream.

"It was the most terrible experience, I assure you. I've been fainting on and off ever since." She sat down in Mrs Brown's easy chair, evidently with every intention of fainting on and off again, when William's father entered.

He greeted Miss Montagu curtly. Mr Brown, though a well-meaning man, wasn't at his best before breakfast.

"Well," he said with one eye sternly fixed on William and the other apprehensively fixed on his visitor, "what's he been doing now?"

"Oh, John," said Mrs Brown, "it's burglars. Miss Montagu's had burglars in the night."

"Three of them," said Miss Montagu with a sob. "Three great giants of men. They've ransacked the place. They've stolen all my jewellery. They – they covered me with revolvers and threatened to take my life. They—"

"Have you told the police?" said Mr Brown, his eye wandering wistfully to the dish cover beneath which reposed his eggs and bacon.

"Yes, they're coming round to interview me. I'm completely unstrung by it. I can't tell you the state I've been in. If I've fainted once I've fainted a dozen times. A gang of masked men. I resisted them and they shot. They missed me, but such was the shock to my nerves that I fainted, and when I returned to consciousness they were gone, but the place was ransacked—"

"Here's a policeman," said Mr Brown cheerfully, "just going into your house. Hadn't you better go and interview him?"

"Oh, fetch him in here, dear Mr Brown. I feel too much upset to move."

Muttering something inaudible beneath his breath and with a long agonised look at the coffee pot and bacon dish, Mr Brown went out to intercept the policeman.

The policeman entered jauntily, taking his notebook out of his pocket.

"It's burglars," said Miss Montagu, wringing her hands and visibly cheered by her increasing audience. "My house was entered last night and I was attacked by a gang of men – masked."

"Was you roused by the noise, Miss?"

"Yes," said Miss Montagu eagerly. "I went down to confront them, and there I found five or six—"

"Five or six?" asked the policeman magisterially.

"Six," said Miss Montagu after a moment's hesitation.

"Six," repeated the policeman, licking his pencil again and beginning to write in his notebook. "Six." He wrote it down with great deliberation and then said a third time, "Six."

"I confronted them," went on Miss Montagu, "but they gagged me and bound me to a chair."

Mr Brown, unable to control any longer the pangs of hunger, had sat down at the table and, with a fine disregard of everyone else in the room, was attacking a large helping of bacon and eggs.

"A chair, did you say, Miss?" said the policeman, brightening as though they had arrived at last at the most important part of the evidence.

"Yes, a chair, of course. They gagged me and bound me to it and then I fainted. When I recovered consciousness I was alone. The house was ransacked. My jewellery gone."

"Ransacked," murmured the policeman, writing hard and moistening his pencil every other second. "Jewellery." He closed his book and assumed his pontifical air. "You've left heverything, I 'ope, as they left it."

Miss Montagu considered this question for a minute in silence. Then she spoke in the tone of voice of one who has been soaring in the clouds and suddenly fallen to earth with a bump. "Oh, no," she said. "Oh, no. I – I tidied up after them."

Mr Brown, who had reached the marmalade stage and was feeling uppish, said, "A

great mistake," and was at once crushed by a glance from the eye of the Law.

"What exactly is missing, Miss?" said the Law pompously.

"I – I can't be quite sure," she said.

The policeman put his notebook into his pocket and squared himself as if for a fight. "I'd better come and visit the scene of the crime with you now, at once, Miss, and collect what evidence I can."

"I'll come with you," said Mrs Brown compassionately to Miss Montagu. "I'm sure you aren't fit to go alone."

"Thank you so much," said Miss Montagu. "I feel that I might faint again any minute."

Led by the policeman and supported by Mrs Brown, she made her way slowly to her own domain. William's father snorted contemptuously and poured himself out another cup of coffee.

Over William's inscrutable countenance there flickered just for one moment a smile . . .

Miss Montagu was resting in her chair in the garden. She had had a tiring day.

She had had a constant stream of visitors who came ostensibly to enquire after her health, but really to elicit the whole thrilling story of the burglary. She felt exhausted, but she had the satisfaction of knowing that nothing was being talked about in the village but her burglary.

Suddenly she looked up. That wretched boy was sitting, actually sitting, on her fence, after all she'd said to him. In his arms he held a nondescript dog that looked as if it had numbered among its ancestors a sheep and a cat and a monkey.

She was just going to order him to descend at once and go in to write to his father again when something attracted her attention.

The dog was wearing a collar. And the boy was looking at her in a meaningful sort of way – a very meaningful sort of way. Then, still looking at her, he took from one pocket a handful of arrows and threw them carelessly down into his garden. From the other pocket he took three balls and began carelessly to play with them.

The words she had meant to say did not come. Instead she said faintly, "W-where did you get those?"

The boy's look became still more meaningful. "From your house," he said, still carelessly playing with his ball, "last night. Don' you remember? I was wearin' a mask an' you was wearin' a pink dressing-gown an' you said you was a poor defenceless woman. And

you told me to think of my wife an' not to do anything rash. Don' you remember?"

Then, apparently losing all interest in the subject, he returned to playing with his ball.

There was a long, long silence – the longest silence Miss Montagu ever remembered in her life. Then, after what seemed to her several hours, she spoke in a small, faraway voice. "They – they'll never believe you."

"Oh," said William casually. "I'm not goin' to tell 'em if – I mean, there's really no reason why I should tell 'em."

There was another long silence – longer even than the first. But during it Miss Montagu's brain worked quickly. She understood what William's "if" had meant.

She looked up at that horrid, freckled, untidy-headed boy who was whistling so unconcernedly upon her fence and said sternly, "How can you tell such an untruth about last night?"

William stopped whistling for a minute and looked at her.

"I hope you won't tell such a silly untruth to anyone else," she said severely. "If you don't – I mean, I mean I was going to tell you that my nerves have quite recovered now and that no noise from your garden will disturb me. Also, if your arrows or things come over here, you may come over and fetch them."

Then, with great dignity, she got up and swept into the house.

William watched her retreat with apparent unconcern. "Thank you," was all he said.

Not Much

William's mother and Ethel, his grown-up sister, were cutting sandwiches in the kitchen.

"Who're you makin' sandwiches for?" William demanded.

His mother surveyed him tentatively. "Well, dear, would you like to help at a little party this afternoon?"

"People comin' to tea?" asked William guardedly.

"Yes, dear, you'd be such a help and—"

"I'll eat up all they leave afterwards for you," he said obligingly, "but I think I won't come this time."

"Thank Heaven!" murmured Ethel.

William crammed a handful of crusts into

his mouth, and went out into the hall. Here he burst suddenly into a flood of raucous sound:

"Oh, who will o'er the downs with me?
Oh, who will with me ri – i – i – i – i – ide?"

Mr Brown opened the library door. "Will – you – stop – that – confounded – noise?"

"I'm sorry," said William amicably. "I forgot you din't like musick."

After lunch, William sallied forth once more into the world.

At a bend in the road he stood silent. A group of children were walking along in front of him. They had evidently just come out of the station.

At their head walked a tall, thin man. The children – boys and girls – were about William's age. They were clean and tidy, but badly dressed and with pale faces. A little girl turned round.

"'Ullo," she said with a friendly grin, "did

yer nearly git left be'ind? Wot's yer name?"

William liked the almost incredible frizziness of her hair. He liked the dirty feather in her hat and the violet blue of her dress. He liked the way she talked. "William," he replied, "Wot's yours?"

"Heglantine," she said. "Nice name, ain't it? Loverly, comin' on the train, weren't it?"

It was evident that she took him for one of her party.

"Um," he said noncommittally.

"Din't see yer on the train. Such a crowd, weren't there? Some from St Luke's an' some from St Mary's. I dunno 'alf of 'em. I were jus' lookin' out for someone to pal up wiv."

William's heart swelled with delight.

A boy in front turned round. He was pale and undersized and wore a loud check cap that would have fitted a grown man. "'Ullo, Freckles!" he said to William.

William glared at him fiercely.

Eglantine quickly interposed. "Nah then, Albert," she said sharply. "You mind wot yer

34

says ter me an' my frens!"

The boy grinned and dropped behind with them. "Wot we goin' ter do, anyways," he said in a mollifying tone of friendship. "Not much ter do in the country, is there?"

"There's games," said William, deliberately adopting the accent of his new friends. He decided to adopt it permanently. He considered it infinitely more interesting than that used by his own circle.

"Games!" said the boy in the check cap with infinite scorn. "Runnin' races an' suchlike. An' lookin' at cows an' pickin' flowers. Thanks! *Not much*!"

William stored up this expression for future use.

"They said, as 'ow there'd be a tea, an' I'm not one ter miss a tea – a proper tea wiv cake an' all – *not much*!"

William was watching the large check cap with fascinated eyes. "Where'd you get that cap?" he said at last.

"Dunno. Like ter swap?"

William nodded. The boy whipped off his cap without a word and handed it to William, taking William's school cap in return.

William with a sigh of bliss, put it on. It enveloped his whole head and forehead, the large peak standing out over his nose. He pulled it firmly down. It was the cap of his dreams – the cap of a brigand chief.

"We are smart, ain't we?" said Eglantine, with a high-pitched laugh.

William felt blissfully happy, walking along beside her.

"'Ere – wot does yer farver do?" demanded Albert of William suddenly.

"Er – wot does yours?" replied William guardedly.

"'E goes round wiv a barrow, sellin' things."

"Mine sweeps chimneys," said Eglantine. "'E gets that black."

They both turned on William. "Wot does yours do?"

William could not bear to confess that his father merely caught a train to London and his office every morning. "Ain't got no father," he said doggedly.

"You're an orphan then," said Eglantine, with an air of wide knowledge of the world.

At this point, the tall, thin man in front stopped and collected his flock around him. He wore a harassed and anxious expression. "Now," he said, "are we all here?"

"Please sir, William's an orphan," said Eglantine excitedly.

"Yes, yes," said the tall man, "poor little

fellow. Now, come along. We're going to play in the woods first, children, and then go to a kind friend's to tea. The Vicar's arranged it all. Very kind! This way, I think."

Again, the little procession moved on its way.

"Softie!" commented Eglantine scornfully. "Why can't they talk like other folks?"

William redoubled his efforts to acquire his friend's intonation.

"Yes, why, I'd like ter know," he said, pulling his large and loud tweed cap yet further over his eyes.

The tall, thin man at the head of the procession stopped again. "I'll just go into this house, children," he said, "and ask the way to the woods." He went up the pathway.

"Are we going to 'ang round *'im* all the time?" asked William discontentedly. "Won't be no fun – *not much*," he added proudly, after a slight pause.

"Well, 'e knows the way an' we don't," said Albert.

"I do," said William. "You come with me – quick – afore he comes out."

They all followed William silently round the back of the house, across a field and along another road.

At a pair of iron gates leading past a lodge into a winding drive, Eglantine stopped. "Let's go in here."

Even William was aghast. "It's someone's garden," he explained, "they'll turn us out."

Eglantine squared her thin shoulders. "Let 'em jus' try turnin' *me* out," she said.

"*Not much*," murmured William proudly.

They went up the drive. Then Eglantine saw a hedge with a gate in it and marshalled her party through that. Within they saw a lawn, some gardens and a fountain.

"Looks all right," commented Eglantine loftily.

A young man rose languidly from a hammock in the trees. "I beg your pardon?" he said politely.

"Granted," said Eglantine, not to be outdone in politeness.

"Can I do anything for you?" said the young man.

"We're St Luke's and St Mary's," explained Eglantine importantly.

"I see," said the young man.

"'Im," said Eglantine, pointing at William, "'e's an orphan."

The young man adjusted a monocle. "Really, how intensely interesting!"

"We've come into the country for a 'oliday," went on Eglantine, "an' we jus' came in 'ere, ter see wot it was like in 'ere."

"How extremely kind of you!" said the young man. "I hope you like it."

Eglantine surveyed the scene distantly. "Wiv a band an' some swings an' an ice-cream cart, it'd be all right."

Most of the children were already making the best of their opportunities. Some were chasing butterflies; some picking flowers; some were paddling in the ornamental pond.

A butler came down the path with an

expression of horror on his face. The young man waved him away. "It's all right, Thomson," he said.

"Yes, sir," said the man, "but her ladyship has arrived, sir. Her ladyship has had her boxes sent upstairs. I thought I'd better warn you, sir."

The young man groaned. "Is there time for me to be summoned to town?" he asked.

"I'm afraid not. She's coming to find you now, sir. Here she is, sir."

A large woman bore down upon them. She wore a large cloak and a large hat, and several Pomeranian dogs trotted at her heels.

The young man rose to receive her.

"Ah! Here you are, Bertram," she said, "you didn't invite me, but I've come."

"How awfully good of you, Aunt," said the young man dispiritedly.

The lady put up her lorgnette spectacles and surveyed the children. "Who – are – these – ragamuffins?" she said slowly and distinctly.

"Oh, just a nice little party of mine," said the young man pleasantly. "St Luke's and St Mary's. You'll get awfully fond of them. They're very loveable."

The lady's face became stony. "Are you aware," she said, "that they're trampling on the flowers, and splashing in the pond, and sitting on the sundial?"

"Oh, yes. Just jolly childish pranks, you know."

"And that one in the awful tweed cap—"

"He's an orphan," said the young man.

"I'm going to give you the room next to his. He's got quite a jolly voice. I heard him humming to himself a moment ago."

One of the girls lifted up her voice in a wail. "Oo – oo – oo – oo. I'm tired of the country. I want to go 'ome. Oo – oo – oo."

Then Eglantine, who had surveyed the visitor in outraged silence for a few moments, at last burst forth. She set her thin hands on her thin hips and began. "An' who're you ter talk about ragamuffins? Queen of England, are yer? An' wot about yer own 'at? Insultin' other people, in other people's gardens."

The five dogs, excited by the uproar, burst into simultaneous yapping.

The lady turned to her nephew. "I'm going straight home, Bertram. When you have a civilised house to invite me to, perhaps you'll let me know."

"Yes, Aunt," he screamed back. "Shall I see you to your car?"

He left them for a few minutes and returned, mopping his brow, in time to rescue three boys from an early death from drowning in the pond.

The butler appeared once more. "There's a gentleman at the front door, sir, who seems in a great state, sir. He says that he's lost some children—"

The young man's face brightened. "Ah," he said, "tell him I've found some. They've done me a very good turn, but I shouldn't mind being relieved of them now."

William was looking anxiously down the road where the tall man was taking them.

Eglantine began to hold forth again. "Look at them 'ouses," she said, with a contemptuous glance at the houses between which they were passing. "Swank! That's all it is. Swank! Livin' in big 'ouses an' talkin' so soft. I've no patience wiv 'em. I wouldn't be one of 'em – not for nuffin."

William was growing more and more uneasy.

The tall man turned in at a gate. William

moistened his lips. "He's making a *mistake*," he murmured, pulling his check cap still further over his eyes.

At the door stood Mrs Brown and Ethel. Their glance fell first on Eglantine.

"Oh, what a dreadful child," whispered Mrs Brown.

Next it fell on all that could be seen of Eglantine's companion.

"What an appalling cap!" whispered Ethel.

"Here we are," said the tall man, with a note of relief in his voice. "It's too kind of you. This is – er – Eglantine, and – er – this little boy is an orphan, poor little chap!"

Mrs Brown laid her hand tenderly on the tweed cap. "Poor little boy," she began. "Poor little—" Then she met the eyes beneath the tweed cap . . .

William sat and glared across the table at his late friend. He felt himself disgraced forever.

He was an outcast, outside the pale, one of the "swanks" who lived in big houses and

talked soft.

His mother's and Ethel's intonation and accent seemed, at that moment, a public humiliation to him. He did not dare to meet Eglantine's eyes.

Fiercely he munched a currant bun. Into his unoccupied hand stole a small grimy one.

"Never mind," whispered Eglantine, "yer can't 'elp it."

And William whispered gratefully, "*Not much*."

That Boy

William had gone away with his family for a holiday, and he was not enjoying it. For one reason, it was not the sea.

William found things monotonous inland. There were no crabs, no rock pools, and nothing to do.

Robert and Ethel, his grown-up brother and sister, had joined a tennis club and were out all day. Not that William had much use for Robert and Ethel. He preferred them out all day, as a matter of fact.

"All I say *is*," he said aggrievedly to his mother, "that no one cares whether *I'm* havin' a nice time or not. I might jus' as well be *dead* for all the trouble some people take to make me happy."

His mother looked at his scowling, freckled countenance.

"Well," she said, "you can go for walks."

"*Walks*!" said William. "It's no use goin' for *walks* without Jumble."

His father lowered his newspaper. "Your arithmetic report was vile," he said. "You might occupy your time with a few sums. I'll set them for you."

William turned upon his parent a glance before which most men would have quailed. Then, with a short and bitter laugh, he turned on his heel and left the room.

He put his head in at the window as he went towards the gate. "I'm goin' out, Mother," he said in a voice which expressed stern sorrow rather than anger.

"All right, dear," said Mrs Brown sweetly.

"I may not be coming back – never," he added darkly.

"All right, dear," said his mother.

William walked down to the village in black dejection. What people came away for holidays *for* beat him. At home there was old Jumble to take for a walk and throw sticks for, and various well-known friends and enemies to make life interesting.

Here – well, he might as well be *dead*.

A motor coach stood outside the post office, and people were taking their places in it. William looked at it contemptuously. He began to listen in a bored fashion to the conversation of two young men.

"I'm awfully glad you ran down," one of them was saying. "To tell you the truth, I'd got so bored that I'd taken a ticket for this coach trip. Can't stand 'em really."

"Will they give you your money back?" said the other.

"It doesn't matter," said the first.

Then he met William's dark, unflinching gaze and said carelessly, "Here, kid, like a ticket for the coach trip?"

William considered the question. This was better than nothing. "All right," he said, "I don't mind going."

An hour later, the coach stopped at a country village. The driver explained that the church was an excellent example of Early Norman architecture. This left William cold. He did not even glance at it.

The driver went on to remark that an excellent meal could be obtained at the village inn. Here William's expression kindled into momentary animation, only to fade again into despair. He had spent his last twopence that morning upon a stick of liquorice.

It had caused a certain amount of friction between himself and his elder brother. William had put it – partially sucked – upon a chair and Robert had come in from tennis and inadvertently sat down upon it. Being in a moist condition, it had stuck to Robert's white flannel trousers.

"Well, I didn't *make* him sit down on it, did

I? He talks about me spoiling his trousers – well, wot about him spoilin' my liquorice? All I say is – who wants to eat it, now he's been sittin' on it?"

Robert had unkindly taken this statement at its face value and thrown the offending stick of liquorice into the fire.

William extricated himself from the coach.

An elderly lady in *pince-nez* looked at him pityingly. "What's the matter, little boy?" she said. "You look unhappy."

William merely smiled bitterly.

"Is your mother with you?" she went on.

"Nope," said William, thrusting his hands into his pockets and scowling.

"Your father, then?"

"Huh!" said William, as though bitterly amused at the idea.

"You surely haven't come alone!"

William gave vent to the dark emotions of his soul. "All I can say *is* that if you knew my family, you'd be jolly glad to go anywhere alone if you was me."

The lady made little clicking noises with her tongue, expressive of sorrow and concern. "Dear, dear, dear!" she said. "And are you going to have tea now?"

William assumed his famous expression of suffering patience. "I've got no money."

"Haven't they given you any money for your tea?" said the lady indignantly.

"Huh! Not *they*!" said William with a bitter laugh. "They wun't of let me come if they'd known. *They* wun't of paid anything for me. It was a frien' gave me the ticket jus' to give me a bit of pleasure," he said pathetically, "but *they* wun't even give me money for my tea."

"You poor child," said the lady. "Come along, *I'll* give you your tea."

"Thanks," said William humbly and gratefully, trudging off with her in the direction of the village inn.

William, generally speaking, had only to say a thing to believe it. He saw himself now as the persecuted victim of a cruel and unsympathetic family, and the picture was not without a certain pleasure.

"I suppose," said the lady uncertainly, as William consumed boiled eggs with relish, "that your family are kind to you."

"You needn't s'pose that," said William, his mouth full of bread and butter, his gaze turned on her lugubriously.

"They surely aren't *cruel* to you?"

"Crule," said William with a shudder, "jus' isn't the word."

The lady leant across the table. "Little boy," she said soulfully, "you must tell me *all*. I want to *help* you. I go about the world helping people, and I'm going to help you. Don't be frightened. You know people can be put in prison for being cruel to children. If I reported the case to the Society for Prevention of Cruelty to Children—"

William was taken aback. "Oh, I wun't like to do that! I wun't like to get 'em in trouble."

"Ah," she said, "but you must think of your happiness, not theirs!"

She watched, fascinated, as William finished a third plate of bread and butter. "I can see you've been starved," she said, "and I could tell at once from your expression that you were unhappy. Have you brothers and sisters?"

William put half a cake into his mouth, before replying. "Two," he said briefly, "one each. Grown-up. But they jus' care about nothin' but their own pleasure. For instance," he went on, warming to his theme, "this morning I bought a few sweets with jus' a bit of money I happened to have, an' he took them from me, and threw them into the fire."

The lady made the sympathetic clicking sound with her tongue. "Dear! Dear! Dear!" she said. "There's generally only one explanation of an unhappy home. I've investigated so many cases. Does your father drink?"

William nodded sadly. "Yes," he said. "That's it."

"Oh," she breathed. "Your *poor* mother!"

But William wanted no divisions of sympathy. "Mother drinks too," he said.

"You *poor*, poor child!"

William wondered whether to make Robert and Ethel drink, too, then decided not to. As an artist, he knew the value of restraint.

"Never mind," said the lady, "you shall have *one* happy afternoon, at any rate."

She took him to the village shop and bought him chocolates, and sweets and bananas.

William found some difficulty in retaining an expression suggestive of an unhappy home life, but he managed it fairly successfully.

He began to feel very tired on the way back. He had a lovely time. He was almost asleep when the coach drew up at the post office. Everyone began to descend.

He took a polite and distant farewell of the elderly lady. But he found that the elderly lady was coming with him. "Where do you live?" she said.

"Oh," said William vaguely, "jus' somewhere along here."

"I'm coming to see your father," said the lady in a determined voice.

William was aghast. "Oh – er – I wun't do that if I was you!" he said.

"I often find," she said, "that a drunkard does not realise what unhappiness he makes in his home. I often find that a few words of warning are taken to heart—"

"You'd better *not*," said William desperately. "He dun't mind *wot* he does! He'll be jus' mad drunk when we get in. You'd better not come *near* our house . . ."

"No, I shan't feel that I've done my duty till I've at any rate tried to make him see his sin."

They were in the street now in which William's family were staying. William looked pale and desperate. He was creeping cautiously and silently past the house by the side of his unsuspecting companion, when a shrill cry reached him.

"William! Hi! William! Where have you been? Mother says come in at once!"

It was Ethel leaning out of an upstairs window. Sadly, he opened the garden gate.

"You'd better not come in," he said faintly,

"he gets *violent*, about this time of day . . ."

Mr Brown looked up from the evening paper as his younger son entered, followed by a tall, thin lady of prim appearance, wearing *pince-nez*.

Mr Brown groaned inwardly. Had William killed her cat or merely broken one of her windows? "Er – good evening," he said.

"Good evening," said the visitor. "I have been spending the afternoon with your boy."

"Very kind of you," murmured Mr Brown.

"He has told me something of the state of

things in his home," burst out the visitor. "I saw at once that he was unhappy and half-starved."

Mr Brown's jaw dropped. William very slowly and cautiously tiptoed to the door.

"He told me about you and his mother. I was sure – I am sure – that you don't realise what your – er – failing means to this innocent child."

Mr Brown raised a hand to his brow.

"Your conscience, you see," said the visitor triumphantly, "troubles you. Why should the memory of childhood mean to that dear boy blows and curses and unkindness – and just because you are a slave to your baser appetites?"

Mr Brown removed his hand from his brow. "You'll pardon my interrupting you," he said, "but perhaps you would be good enough to give me some slight inkling of what you are talking about."

"Ah, you *know*," she said fervently. "Why pretend? I had the dear child's company all afternoon and know what he has suffered."

Here Mrs Brown entered and the visitor turned to her. "And you," she went on. "Can you – won't you – give up for the sake of your child?" Her voice quivered with emotion.

"I think, my dear," said Mr Brown, "that you had better send for a doctor. This lady is not well."

"But who *is* she?" said Mrs Brown.

"I don't know – she's someone William found."

The lady flung out her arms. "Won't you?

Can't you – for the sake of your own happiness, as well as his – give it up?"

They stared at her.

"Madam," said Mr Brown despairingly, "what do you wish us to give up?"

"*Drink*," she answered dramatically.

Mr Brown sat down heavily. "*Drink*!" he echoed.

Mrs Brown gave a little scream. "*Drink*!" she said. "But we're teetotallers."

It was the turn of the visitor to sit down heavily. "Surely," she said, "that boy did not deceive me!"

"Madam," said that boy's father bitterly, "it is more than probable."

When the visitor, protesting, apologising and still not quite convinced, had been seen off the premises, Mr Brown turned grimly to his wife. "Now," he said, "where is that boy?"

But William had quietly slipped away, having decided that going for a walk, even without Jumble, wasn't a bad idea after all.

Aunt Arabelle
in Charge

The news that Ginger's parents were going abroad for a fortnight was received by Ginger and his friends, the Outlaws, with an exhilaration that they strove in vain to hide.

"We'll have the conservatory for our jungle camp," said Ginger.

"And we'll play Alpine sports on the front stairs," said William.

"We can get up a bear hunt with the rug from the drawing-room," said Douglas.

"And we can have a *fine* time with those African weapons in your father's dressing-room," said Henry.

Ginger, not wishing to seem too unfilial, added, "I'm sorry they're goin', of course, but it isn't as if they weren't comin' back."

"An', after all, it's only a fortnight," said Henry, "an' we'll put all the things back again so's they'll never know we've had them."

Their exhilaration was slightly damped when they heard that an aunt of Ginger's, who had not seen Ginger since he was a baby, was coming to keep house in his parents' absence.

"If she's like *some* aunts—" said William, speaking with gloom and bitterness from an exhaustive acquaintance with those relatives.

"She may be all right," said Ginger. "She writes things for papers."

The spirits of the Outlaws rose again. They had met several people who wrote things for papers and had found them refreshingly absent-minded and conveniently blind to their immediate surroundings.

"She'll prob'ly never notice what we're doin'," said William. "If she's like some of 'em she'll watch us doin' Alpine sports down the front stairs an' never know we're there at all."

"I hope so," said Ginger, "'cause my mother will give me ten shillings when she comes back, if my aunt says I've been good."

They showed signs of interest and excitement at his news. It was the custom of the Outlaws to have all things in common, especially tips.

"Oh, we'll get that ten shillin's all right," said William confidently. "She'll be so busy writin' soppy tales that she'll be as good as blind an' deaf."

The appearance of Ginger's aunt was certainly reassuring.

She was a small, short-sighted woman with ink-stained fingers and untidy hair. She took her duties in what Ginger considered a very proper spirit.

"I'm a busy woman, dear boy," she said to him, "and I simply can't be disturbed at my work, so you must try not to bother me with *anything*. Just look after yourself and solve your own little problems as best you can. There's no reason why we should trouble each other except in case of an absolute *crisis*."

So Ginger looked after himself and solved his own little problems and on the whole solved them very well.

The problems consisted chiefly of how to turn the conservatory into a jungle, how to organise a really good bear hunt with the aid of the drawing-room hearth rug and Ginger's father's treasured collection of African spears, and how to make the staircase into a satisfactory Alpine sports ground.

The last problem was solved by placing mattresses down the length of the staircase.

William and Ginger became expert skiers, Henry was content to climb up and down with the aid of Ginger's father's alpenstock, and Douglas's speciality was rolling down it inside an empty linen basket.

William, who had written a play that had been acted by his followers and a serial story that had been published in a newspaper of his

editorship, and who therefore considered himself a fully fledged member of the profession of letters, took a great interest in Aunt Arabelle's activities.

"You tell her I'll help her if she gets stuck in a tale," he said to Ginger. "Tell her I'm jolly good at writin' tales. Well, I've never read a better tale than that one I wrote called *The Bloody Hand*."

"I have," said Ginger.

"I bet you haven't," said William. "It's the best tale anyone's ever written. I wrote it, so I ought to know."

It occurred to William that it would be a kind action if he added a few helpful touches to Aunt Arabelle's manuscript while she was out taking her daily constitutional, as a pleasant surprise for her on her return.

"I bet I can write about ghosts moanin' an' rattlin' chains as well as anyone," he said.

"P'raps she doesn't write that sort of tale," objected Ginger.

"Then I can write about dead bodies and findin' who killed 'em."

"There's other sorts of tales," said Ginger.

"No, there isn't," said William firmly, "not that anyone ever wants to read, anyway."

But an exhaustive search of Aunt Arabelle's desk revealed no stories of any sort – only a typewritten sheet headed, *Answers to Correspondents*. The first was "I'm sorry, dear, that he has not spoken yet, but just go on being your own sweet self, and I am sure he will soon."

"What's that mean?" said Ginger with a mystified frown.

"It's someone who's got a dumb child an' is tryin' to cure it," explained William in all good faith. "What's the next?"

"'I understand so well, Pansy dear,'" read on Douglas, "'the anguish and turmoil that lives beneath the brave front you turn to the world. Probably he feels the same. Couldn't you find some mutual friend to introduce you? Then I am sure all will be well.'"

"What's that mean?" said Ginger, looking more mystified.

William himself looked puzzled for a minute. Finally enlightenment seemed to come. "It's someone what's got stomach-ache an' she's tellin' 'em to get to know a doctor what's got stomach-ache too, so's he'll know how to cure her. It's a jolly good idea. I often wish our doctor had a stomach-ache when I have it. I bet he'd try 'n' find a nicer medicine if he'd gotter take it himself."

The next day William boldly tackled Aunt Arabelle on her literary work, kindly offering to give his help if she wished to turn her art into fiction. "I've written some jolly good tales," he said, "an' I wouldn't mind helpin' you a bit."

"No, thank you, dear boy," said Aunt Arabelle. "You see, I don't go in for fiction."

"It's much more interestin' than writin' to people about dumbness an' stomach-ache," said William.

"But I don't do that, dear. I help them in their little troubles of the heart."

"Well, I think diseases are all dull," said William, "whether they're heart or stomach-ache or anything else. What do you write them for?"

"For a little paper called *Woman's Sphere*. I don't only do the *Answers to Correspondents*, of course. I sometimes do interviews. But," she sighed, "it's difficult to get really interesting people to be interviewed for the *Woman's Sphere*. It's only a two-penny, you see."

But William, whose literary experience was confined to fiction, had lost interest in her work though, liking always to be up to date, he made a mental note that *Answers to Correspondents* should form a part of the next paper he edited.

"I don't think much of her," he said to Ginger, "writing rot like that about hearts an' stomachs an' dumbness an' things."

"She's better than any of your aunts, anyway," said Ginger, feeling that the honour of his family must be defended.

"Oh, is she?" said William, accepting the challenge. "All right, you tell me one of my aunts she's better than."

"The one that asked why they only used one goal-post at a time when she came to see the rugger match."

"Oh, is she? Well, let me tell you she's not. I'd sooner have her than one that writes about hearts an' stomachs an' dumbness."

"An' the one that told your father it was wrong to take life in any form and greenfly had as much right to existence as he had?"

The argument degenerated from this point

into a discussion on aunts in general and finally took the form of rivalry for strangeness in aunts from which Ginger emerged triumphant with Aunt Arabelle.

The pursuits, however, that had been so exciting during the first few days of her visit soon began to pall.

The conservatory had its limitations as a jungle, the hunt with spears proved interesting only to a certain point (spears were unwieldy weapons and prone to bite the hand that fed them), and, though Alpine sports on the staircase retained their charm the longest, their delights too were exhausted before the end of the first week.

Then the Outlaws began to look round for fresh interests. They were torn between a desire to return to the woods and fields that were the usual scenes of their activities, and a feeling that to leave house and garden of Ginger's home in the present circumstances was to waste a golden opportunity that might never occur again.

For Aunt Arabelle, shut in the library, writing her *Answers to Correspondents* and articles on *How to Beautify the Home* or *Feed the Husband* or *Renovate the Wardrobe on a Small Income*, remained blind and deaf to all their doings, and the domestic staff of Ginger's home had long since washed its hands of him.

"Let's think of something *really* exciting to do," said William.

It was Ginger who thought of it.

"Let's have a sea fight in the conservatory with paper boats an' sticks to guide 'em," he said. "We can turn on the tap enough to have the floor jus' under water, an' the floor's made of tiles so it won't do it any harm, an' we won't have enough to go up the step into the hall."

The idea was adopted eagerly by the Outlaws, and they set to work at once making fleets of paper boats. Then they flooded the conservatory.

They found that as the "sea" trickled out

72

beneath the door into the garden it was necessary to replenish it at frequent intervals.

It was Ginger's idea to leave the tap on – "Just enough to keep a decent sea" – and, in the excitement of the ensuing naval conflict, they did not notice that the tap had been left on too full and that the water was rising above the step into the hall.

Aunt Arabelle, a faraway smile on her lips (she had just written a very beautiful little article on the *Art of the Love Letter*), stepped from the study to the hall and was brought down to earth abruptly by finding herself standing in a large pool of water.

It struck cold and clammy through the moccasins that she always wore when she was working. It swirled round her ankles. Aunt Arabelle clutched her skirts about her in terror, and, without stopping to consider the particular element that was threatening her, shouted, "Fire!"

The cook rushed out from the kitchen with the fire extinguisher, and, as she had com-

pletely lost her head and as Aunt Arabelle was still shouting "Fire!", proceeded to drench Aunt Arabelle with its contents.

The Outlaws heard the commotion and hastily turned off the tap. But it was too late. Aunt Arabelle had been roughly shaken out of the hazy vagueness in which she usually lived. Some of the contents of the fire extinguisher had gone into her mouth and the taste was not pleasant. The apple-green smock in which she always worked was ruined.

In short, the "absolute crisis" had arrived in which she had decreed that she and Ginger should trouble each other.

"I can't *possibly* tell your mother you've been good now," she said to Ginger.

The Outlaws, who in the intervals of devising the new games had planned the spending of Ginger's good conduct money to the last farthing – and had even spent some of it on credit at the local sweet shop – were aghast. They used their utmost powers of persuasion on Aunt Arabelle but in vain.

"I can't possibly," said Aunt Arabelle simply. "I'd be telling an untruth if I said that Ginger had been good, and I couldn't *possibly* tell an untruth."

It was a point of view from which they found it impossible to shake her. Gloom descended upon them. Even the house had lost its charms.

They walked down into the village, carefully avoiding the local sweet shop. And in the village they met Anthony Martin.

They saw a little boy of about six, picturesquely attired, wearing a complacent expression and hair that was just too long. He was a stranger to the locality.

"Who are you?" said William.

"Don't you know?" said the little boy with a self-conscious smile. "I'm Anthony Martin."

William's face remained blank. The little boy seemed disappointed by their reception of the information. "Don't you know Anthony Martin?" he said.

"No. Never heard of him," said Ginger.

A shade of contempt came into the little boy's face. "Good heavens!" he said. "Whatever sort of books do you read?"

"Pirates an' Red Indian stories," said William.

The boy looked pained and disgusted. "Good *heavens*!" he said again. "I shouldn't have thought there was *anyone* – Haven't you read any of the Anthony Martin books?"

"No," said William unimpressed. "Did you write 'em? I've written books myself."

"No, my mother writes them, but they're about me. Poems and stories. All about me. Nearly half a million copies have been sold, and they've been translated into fourteen different languages. I've had my photograph in literally hundreds of papers. *Good* papers, I mean. Not rubbish. They're *literary* stories and poems, you know. Really cultured people buy them for their children. There were several Anthony Martin parties in London last year. *Hundreds* of children came. Just to see me. Have you *really* never heard of me?"

William had never met anyone like this before, and he was for the time being too much taken aback to do himself justice. He merely gasped, "No . . . never."

"You can't know much about *books* then," went on the child scornfully, "and your people can't either, or they'd have bought them for you. They're *the* children's classic nowadays. I have *hundreds* of letters from people who've read them. People I've never met. They send me presents at Christmas, too. And—"

"Why have you come here?" said William, stemming the flood.

"My mother's come for a rest," said Anthony Martin. "She's been overworking. And people have been rushing us so. I've got *sick* of Anthony Martin parties. But it seems unkind to disappoint people, and they do so love to see me. We're going to spend a very quiet fortnight down here. I'm not going to give any interviews. Except perhaps one. The editor of *The Helicon* wants to send someone down, and I've half promised to be photographed on her knee. Of course, I don't *quite* know whether I shall yet. Well, I must go home to lunch now. Tell your people you've seen me. They'll be interested. I simply can't understand your never having heard of me. Good morning."

The Outlaws stood open-mouthed and watched Anthony Martin's small, dapper figure as it strolled nonchalantly away. Then they turned gloomily homeward. The incident had increased their depression. They found Aunt Arabelle dried and changed and in a state of great excitement.

"My dears!" she said. "You'll never *guess* who's come to stay in the village. Anthony Martin!"

"We've seen him," said William dejectedly.

"But, my dears, aren't you *thrilled*?"

"No," said William.

"You know his *sweet* stories, don't you?"

"No," said William.

"Oh, I must read some to you. I've got them all here. I never go anywhere without them."

The dejection of the Outlaws deepened.

"You've actually *seen* him?" went on Aunt Arabelle eagerly.

"Yes."

"Oh, my dears, I *must* see him. I wonder – no, I suppose it would be *impossible*—"

"What?" said Ginger.

"I have written several times officially, and I've had no answer. Of course, the *Woman's Sphere* isn't *quite* . . . I mean, they can't be *expected* . . . but he does give interviews quite a lot."

"Oh, yes," said Ginger, "he said he was doing that. Being photographed on someone's knee."

"Oh, *lucky* someone!" said Aunt Arabelle ecstatically. "Did he say what paper?"

"Sounded like a pelican," said William.

"*The Helicon*," said Aunt Arabelle humbly. "Ah, yes, of course . . ." And she sighed deeply, wistfully.

William looked at her, and the ghost of the lost ten shillings glimmered faintly on his mental horizon. "Do you want him to interview you very much?" he said.

"The other way round, dear boy. I want him to grant *me* an interview with *him*. More than anything else in the world."

"Do you know where he's staying?" said William.

"I heard that they'd taken Honeysuckle Cottage," said Aunt Arabelle. "I must try to get a *peep* at him anyway."

When Anthony Martin strolled out into the garden of Honeysuckle Cottage after tea, he found the four Outlaws standing in a row at the gate.

Anthony Martin was accustomed to people's hanging about to catch a glimpse of him and took it as his right, but the Outlaws' ignorance had piqued his vanity. He strolled up to them slowly.

"I simply can't make out how you've never come across those books," he said. "They're *everywhere*. All the bookshops are full of them. There was my photograph in nearly all the bookshops last Christmas. And there was an Anthony Martin Christmas card. Why, I could go out to tea every day of the year if I wanted to."

"Look here," said William, making himself the spokesman, "will you give an interview to Ginger's aunt? It's a *very* important paper."

"We'll let you play Red Indians with us if you will," said Ginger.

"We'll show you the best place for fishing," said Henry.

"We'll take you to our secret place in the woods," said Douglas.

"Good *heavens*!" said Anthony Martin contemptuously. "That sort of thing doesn't appeal to me in the *least* . . . What's the paper?"

"It's called *The Woman Spear*," said Ginger.

"Never heard of it. What sort of thing does it go in for?"

"Dumbness and stomach-ache and heart

disease and things like that," said William.

"I've never given an interview to a medical paper before," said Anthony Martin importantly. "Look here, our agent's coming over to see us tomorrow. I'll ask him. He knows all about these papers. Come here this time tomorrow, and I'll let you know."

So high had the hopes of the Outlaws risen in the interval that by the time they assembled at the gate of Honeysuckle Cottage the next evening, they had borrowed sixpence from Victor Jameson on the strength of the ten shillings and made new and revised arrangements for the expenditure of the rest.

The small and picturesque figure swaggered down to them through the dusk.

"Well?" said Ginger eagerly.

"It's a jolly good paper," said William, "it's got better stuff on dumbness and stomach-ache and heart disease than any other paper going."

"We'd give you sixpence of it," said Henry,

referring to the ten shillings and forgetting that Anthony Martin didn't know about it.

"We'll show you a tit's nest," said Douglas.

Anthony Martin dismissed the whole subject with a wave of his hand. "It's absolutely off," he said. "Our agent says that it's a piffling paper and that I mustn't on *any* account give an interview to it. It hasn't even any circulation to speak of."

"It does speak of circulation," said

William, pugnaciously, "it's included in heart disease."

"You don't know what you're talking about," said Anthony Martin lightly. "Our agent says it isn't a medical paper at all. It's a two-penny rag."

"It wouldn't do you any harm jus' to give her an interview," pleaded Ginger.

"My dear boy, it would," said Anthony Martin. "It would cheapen our market, and that's the last thing we want to do. Anyway, my mother said you could come to tea tomorrow if you liked."

"Thanks awfully," said William with a fairly good imitation of politeness.

"I want to show you some of our press cuttings," said Anthony Martin. It was clear that he felt a true missionary zeal to convert them to his cult. "Don't bring your aunt," he warned them, "because I shan't see her. And it's no use your telling her things I say because she can't use them without our permission."

*

Next day the Outlaws presented themselves, clean and tidy, at Honeysuckle Cottage.

They were first of all taken to Anthony Martin's mother, who lay on a sofa in the front room with the blinds down, garbed in an elaborate rest gown, her head swathed in a sort of turban. She raised a limp hand in protest as they entered.

"On tiptoe, please, boys. Every sound goes through my head. I'm always like this between the visits of my creative genius. Prostrated. No one knows what I suffer . . ."

The limp hand raised a pair of lorgnettes from among the folds of the elaborate rest gown, and she surveyed the four in silence for several moments. The result of her inspection seemed to deepen her gloom.

"How *sweet* of him to ask you," was her final comment. "I hope you realise that hundreds of people would give almost *anything* for the privilege. I hope you will remember this afternoon all your lives . . ."

The limp hand had dismissed them with an

airy wave, then went to her suffering head as the Outlaws clumped their way out.

Upstairs, Anthony Martin had a suite all to himself, consisting of a small sitting-room, a small drawing-room, and a small bedroom. This self-contained kingdom was presided over by a crushed-looking creature in a cap and apron whom Anthony Martin addressed as "Nurse", and treated with the disdain of an Oriental ruler.

"I want you to hear my latest record first," he said to his guests. "Mother's having records made of the Anthony Martin poems recited by me. She's going to give four very select Anthony Martin parties when we get back to London and she's having the records made for that. They're not being issued to the public yet. This is *Homework*. It's a very popular one. Every verse ends with 'Anthony Martin is doing his sums'."

He put on the record, and the Outlaws listened to it in a dejected silence.

"I'm making another one tomorrow," went

on Anthony Martin when it was finished. "A man's coming in from Hadley with the thing, and I recite into it, and then they make the record from the impression. I'm going to do *Walking in the Puddle* tomorrow. Mother likes me to be quite alone with her when I recite them for records. Anyone else in the room disturbs the atmosphere."

He took down a large album and gave it to William. "You can look at the press cuttings, and I'll take the others into my bedroom and show them the toys that come in the stories. You can go downstairs and fetch up the tea now, Nurse."

William was left alone in the little sitting-room with the album of press cuttings. He turned the pages idly.

Suddenly the door opened, and a man entered carrying a kind of gramophone. "As the front door was open," he said, "I came straight up with this 'ere. It wasn't wanted till tomorrow, but as I was over with something for the Vicarage I thought I'd leave it."

He looked at William in surprise. "You aren't the young gent, are you?"

"No," said William hastily, "he's in his bedroom."

"Well, never mind botherin' him," said the man, "jus' tell 'im I've brought it. I'll explain 'ow it works in case they've forgotten. It's all ready for takin' the impression an' all they have to do is pull out this 'ere and that lets the sound through to the wax. Then take out the finished impression, 'ere, and bring it down to us an' we'll fix it up."

He looked round the room and finally set down the instrument behind a small settee. "That's nice an' out of the way till they want it tomorrow, isn't it?"

Then he creaked downstairs and out of the open front door, leaving William gloomily turning over the pages of the album.

The crushed-looking nurse brought up the tea and the six of them took their places round the table.

Anthony Martin alone sustained the conversation. He had still a lot to tell his new friends, still a lot to show them. He had a letter signed by a Royal Personage. He had a present sent to him by the wife of a Cabinet Minister. He had a photograph of himself taken with an eminent literary Celebrity.

The crushed-looking nurse interrupted this monologue to say, "Now drink up your milk, Master Anthony."

"Shan't," said the world-famous infant.

"You know the doctor told your mother you'd got to drink a glass of milk every tea-time."

"You shut up," said the winsome child.

"Your mother said I wasn't to let you get up from tea till you'd had it," said the nurse.

Anthony Martin turned on her with a torrent of invective which showed that, as far as mastery over words and their fitness for the occasion was concerned, he had inherited much of his mother's literary talent.

During it William remembered that he had forgotten to tell them about the man with the

gramophone. Then a sudden light seemed to shine from his face.

He slipped from the room and returned in a few minutes, leaving the door ajar, ostentatiously flourishing his handkerchief and muttering, "Sorry, left it in there."

Anthony Martin proceeded undisturbed with his scene, his voice upraised shrilly, "Shan't drink it up. All right, you try to make me, you old hag. I'll throw it in your nasty old face. I'll kick your nasty old shins. I'll stamp on your nasty old toes. You leave me alone, I tell you, you old cat, you! I'll tell my mother. Do you think I'm going to do what you tell me now I'm famous all over the world? I—"

It went on for five or ten minutes. William sat listening with a smile on his face that puzzled the others.

It ended by Anthony Martin not drinking his milk and the nurse feebly threatening to tell his mother when she felt better.

After tea, William asked if he might still go on reading the press cuttings and if Ginger might look at them with him as he was sure that Ginger would enjoy them.

Anthony Martin was also sure that Ginger would enjoy them. "I'll leave you to read them here," he said, "and I'll finish showing the other two the things in my bedroom, and then they can read the cuttings and I'll show you the things upstairs."

The other Outlaws were still more puzzled by William's attitude. They felt that he was pandering to this atrocious child without getting them anywhere. They followed his lead as ever, though in a reluctant hangdog fashion that was small tribute to Anthony Martin's much famed "charm".

Douglas and Henry followed him gloomily into the little bedroom that had the nature of an Anthony Martin museum (Anthony Martin's mother took the stage properties with them even on short visits), leaving Ginger and William sitting side by side on the little settee, their heads bent over the album of press cuttings.

As soon as the door had closed on them, William sprang up, dived behind the settee and emerged with something that he held beneath his coat.

"When he comes down tell him I don't feel well and I've gone home," he said, and slipped from the room, leaving Ginger mystified but cheered, for it was evident that William's fertile brain had evolved a plan.

The man at the gramophone shop down in Hadley received him and his precious burden

without suspicion.

"Oh, yes," he said, "tell them I'll have it ready first thing tomorrow. You'll call for it? Very good. An honour for the neighbourhood to have the little gentleman here, isn't it?"

William agreed without enthusiasm and departed.

He was at the gramophone shop early the next morning. He looked rather anxious, and his posture as he entered the shop suggested the posture of one prepared for instant flight. But

evidently nothing had happened in the mean-
time to give him away.

The gramophone man was depressed but
not suspicious. "I think it's a mistake," he
said, as he handed the record over to William.
"It's quite out of his usual line and personally
I don't think it'll be popular. It's not the sort
of thing the public cares for."

William seized his parcel and escaped. At
the end of the street he met the crushed-
looking nurse. She recognised him and
stopped.

"Where's the gramophone shop?" she said.

William, still poised for flight, pointed it
out to her.

"They sent the thing up," she complained,
"a day before we asked for it an' without
leavin' no word an' without the proper thing
in. We've only jus' come across it behind the
settee. An' there's no telephone in the house
so I've got to traipse down here. Would you
like to come back with me and carry it up?"

"I'm frightfully sorry," said William, "but

I'm very busy this morning."

He just caught the bus from Hadley. There wasn't another one for half an hour. That gave him half an hour's start.

Aunt Arabelle had gone out for the morning constitutional (she called it "communing with Nature") that gave her the necessary inspiration for her day's work.

The Outlaws were waiting for him at Ginger's gate and accompanied him at a run to Honeysuckle Cottage. Anthony Martin was strolling aimlessly and sulkily about the garden.

"Hello," he said. Then to William, "Are you better?"

"Yes, thanks," said William.

"I expect you aren't used to such a good tea as you got yesterday," said Anthony Martin and added morbidly, "I'm sick of the country. There's nothing to do in it. It's all very well for writing poems about, but it's rotten to stay in. Mother made up a ripping one last night called *Staying in the Country*. Every verse ends 'Anthony Martin is milking a cow'. She's prostrated again today, of course."

"Will you come over to Ginger's house?" said William. "We've got something to show you there."

The disgust on Anthony Martin's face deepened.

"It's likely *you'd* have anything I'd want to see," he said. "It's your aunt wants to see me, an' I'm jolly well not going to let her."

"No, she's out," said Ginger, "an' it's something you'll be jolly interested in."

"Is it about ME?" said Anthony Martin.

"Yes," said Ginger.

Anthony Martin shrugged petulantly. "I'm always being shown things in the papers about myself that I ought to have seen first," he said. "The press cutting agencies are so abominably slack." He threw a bored glance round the garden. "Well, I may as well come as stay here, I suppose, as long as your aunt isn't there."

It was a relief to have secured him before

the crushed-looking nurse arrived back with her sensational news.

Anthony Martin accompanied them to Ginger's house, giving them as they went his frank views on the country and the people who lived in it. They received his views in silence.

"Well, what is it?" he said as he entered Ginger's house.

"It's a gramophone record," said William.

"Something of mine?"

"Yes."

He followed them into the morning-room, where a gramophone stood on a table by the window. In silence William put a record on.

There came a grating sound, then a shrill voice tempestuously upraised, "Shan't drink it up. All right, you try to make me, you old hag. I'll throw it in your nasty old face. I'll kick your nasty old shins. I'll stamp on your nasty old toes. You leave me alone, I tell you, you old cat, you! I'll tell my mother. D'you think I'm going to do what you tell me now I'm famous all over the world . . ."

There was, of course, a lot more in the same strain. Though not the sweet, flute-like voice of the record *Homework*, it was unmistakably Anthony Martin's voice.

Anthony Martin's aplomb dropped from him. He turned a dull, beet red. His eyes protruded with anger and horror. His mouth hung open.

He made a sudden spring towards the gramophone, but Ginger and Henry caught him and held him in an iron grip while Douglas took off the record and William put it in a cupboard, locked it and pocketed the key.

"Now what are you going to do?" said William.

The result was a continuation of the record with some picturesque additions.

"It's no use going on like that," said William sternly. "We've got it, and everyone'll know it's you all right even if they've never heard you go on like that."

"It's illegal," screamed Anthony Martin.

"I'll go to the police about it. It's stealing."

"All right, go to the police," said William. "I'll hide it where neither the police nor anyone else can find it. And I'll take jolly good care that a lot of people hear it. Ginger's aunt's having a party here this afternoon, and they'll hear it first thing. I bet that in a week everyone'll know about it."

Anthony Martin burst into angry sobs. He stamped and kicked and bit and scratched, but Ginger and Henry continued to hold him in the iron grip.

"Now, listen to us," said William at last. "This is the only record, and we'll give it to you so that you can break it up or throw it away on one condition."

"What's that?" said Anthony Martin.

"That you give Ginger's aunt an interview for her paper, and have your photograph taken sittin' on her knee, same as you were going to for the other."

There was a long silence, during which Anthony Martin wrestled with his professional pride.

Finally, he gulped and said, "All right, you beasts, give it to me."

"When you've given my aunt the interview," said Ginger.

When Ginger's aunt returned, Ginger met her on the doorstep.

"He's here," he said. "And he's goin' to give you an interview for your paper, and he's to have his photograph taken on your knee. He's rung up the photographer in Hadley to do it, and he'll be here any time now."

All the rest of the day, Aunt Arabelle had to keep pinching herself to make sure that she was awake.

"Oh my dears, it's too wonderful to be true. So sweet, isn't he? Such a lesson to all you boys. The things he said in the interview brought tears to my eyes. I only wished you boys loved beauty as that little child does. Oh, it's a wonderful interview. The Editor will simply die of joy when she gets it."

William fixed her with a stony gaze. "We took a jolly lot of trouble gettin' him to give it to you."

"Oh, I'm sure you did, dear boys, and I'm so grateful."

"Er – that tap, that Ginger left on by mistake . . ."

There was a long silence, during which Aunt Arabelle and William looked at each other. And the connection between the tap and the interview dawned gradually upon Aunt Arabelle's simple mind.

"Well, of course, when one comes to think of it, no actual harm was done. In fact, really, it was no more than just washing out the floor of the conservatory and hall. No, Ginger dear, on thinking the matter over, I see nothing in that episode to justify me making any complaints to your parents."

Aunt Arabelle stayed for the night of Ginger's parents' return. She poured out her news in a turgid stream.

"Anthony Martin, you know. *The* Anthony Martin. Yes. Here, a whole half hour's interview. And the Editor was so pleased that she paid me double my usual terms, and she's going to give me all the important interviews now, and she's raised my rate of payment for all my work."

"How splendid," said Ginger's mother. "And has Ginger been good?"

The eyes of Ginger and Aunt Arabelle met in a glance of complete understanding.

"Perfectly good," said Aunt Arabelle,

"quite a help, in fact."

"I'm so glad," said Ginger's mother.

"You said, ten shillings . . ." Ginger reminded her casually.

She took a ten-shilling note out of her purse and handed it to him.

"And now, Ginger dear, I want to tell you about some of the wonderful cathedrals we've seen . . ."

But Ginger had already slipped out to join the other Outlaws, who were waiting for him at the garden gate.